WORLDWIDE ADVENTURES 5

The Amazing Mexican
Secret

CATCH FLAT STANLEY'S
WORLDWIDE ADVENTURES:

The Mount Rushmore Calamity

The Great Egyptian Grave Robbery

The Japanese Ninja Surprise

The Intrepid Canadian Expedition

The Amazing Mexican Secret

AND DON'T MISS ANY OF THESE
OUTRAGEOUS STORIES:

Flat Stanley: His Original Adventure!

Stanley and the Magic Lamp

Invisible Stanley

Stanley's Christmas Adventure

Stanley in Space

Stanley, Flat Again!

FLAT STANLEY's WORLDWIDE ADVENTURES BOOK No. 5

The Amazing Mexican Secret

CREATED BY Jeff Brown
WRITTEN BY Josh Greenhut
PICTURES BY Macky Pamintuan

SCHOLASTIC INC.
New York Toronto London Auckland
Sydney Mexico City New Delhi Hong Kong

ISBN 978-0-545-31193-9

Text copyright © 2010 by the Trust u/w/o Richard C. Brown a/k/a Jeff Brown f/b/o Duncan Brown. Illustrations by Macky Pamintuan, copyright © 2010 by HarperCollins Publishers. All rights reserved. Published by Scholastic Inc., 557 Broadway, New York, NY 10012, by arrangement with HarperCollins Children's Books, a division of HarperCollins Publishers. SCHOLASTIC and associated logos are trademarks and/or registered trademarks of Scholastic Inc.

12 11 10 9 8 7 6 5 4 3 2 1   10 11 12 13 14 15/0

Printed in the U.S.A.   40

First Scholastic printing, September 2010

Typography by Alison Klapthor

CONTENTS

The Amazing Mexican
Secret

¡Olé!

"You have met your match!" Stanley Lambchop called down the hallway to his younger brother, Arthur.

Arthur snorted and stomped his foot.

"My *amigo* is right!" said Carlos, their friend from next door who had slept over. Stanley knew that *amigo* meant "friend" in Spanish. "You will never defeat a great matador—and cape—like us!"

Carlos took Stanley's hands and dangled him just off the ground. This was not very difficult, because Carlos was quite tall for his age. Also, Stanley was only half an inch thick.

Stanley had been flat ever since the enormous bulletin board over his bed fell on him one night while he was sleeping. Sometimes he found being flat no fun at all. People had a habit of sitting on him on the bus. But there were good things about being flat, too. Stanley could slide under doors. He could travel inexpensively through the mail. And he could be a very good bullfighter's cape whenever Carlos came over to play.

Arthur charged down the hall, headed straight for them. At the very last moment, Carlos swung Stanley upward. Arthur passed below as Stanley's toes brushed the ceiling.

"¡Olé!" Carlos and Stanley cried triumphantly. They turned to face their opponent.

Arthur narrowed his eyes and slowly backed up to the other end of the hall.

Stanley knew to take his brother very seriously when Arthur was mad.

After all, it wasn't always easy for Arthur, having a brother who was flat and could do so many unusual things. Plus, Stanley was dressed all in red, which Carlos said made bulls angry.

With a roar, Arthur rushed toward them. He was the fastest bull Stanley had ever seen in their house. Carlos tightened his grip on Stanley's hands.

Stanley took a deep breath and—

"BOYS!!" a voice bellowed right behind them as Carlos swept Stanley through the air.

It was Mr. Lambchop! Stanley was about to swing right into him!

Stanley pointed his toes as hard as he could. They skidded against the ceiling, bringing him to a stop.

The good news was that Stanley Lambchop had not crashed into his father. The bad news was that he was now upside down and face-to-face with him.

"Haven't I told you, 'No horsing around?!'" Mr. Lambchop said.

"But we weren't playing horses, Dad!" protested Arthur.

Mrs. Lambchop appeared from the kitchen. "Arthur is right, dear," she said. "One shouldn't call it horseplay when they were playing bullfight." Stanley's parents were very much in favor of proper speech whenever possible.

"My cousin Carmen del Junco is a

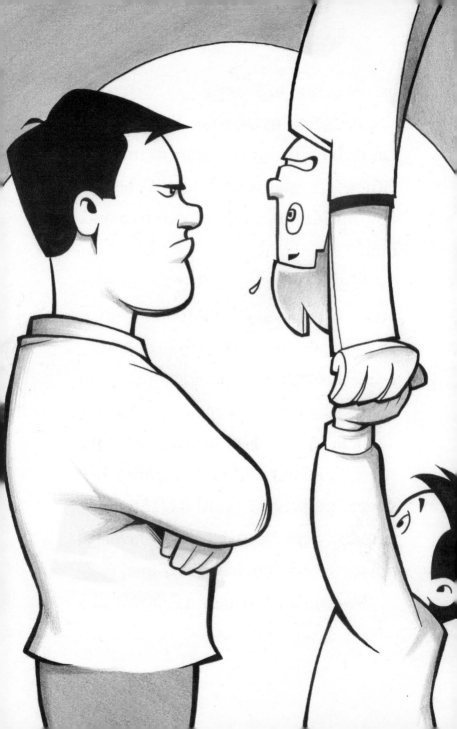

famous matador in Mexico," Carlos admitted. "It is in my blood."

"Speaking of Mexico," Mrs. Lambchop said, smiling, "guess what's for breakfast."

Everyone followed her into the kitchen. "What is it?" Stanley asked, poking the yellow mound on his plate with a fork. It certainly smelled good.

"Why, it's *huevos rancheros*!" Mrs. Lambchop said.

"Looks more like eggs," said Arthur.

Carlos chuckled. "*Huevos* means 'eggs' in Spanish. *Huevos rancheros* is a special dish with eggs on top of a tortilla." He elbowed Stanley. "You will like the tortilla, *amigo*. It is flat like you!"

Everybody dug in.

"Ish ish delishish!" exclaimed Arthur.

"Please don't talk with your mouth full, Arthur," Mr. Lambchop said. "Harriet, you've outdone yourself. These *huevos rancheros* are delicious."

Stanley couldn't agree more, so he shoveled another forkful into his mouth.

"I made it with the seasoning that Carlos's mother gave me," Mrs. Lambchop explained proudly. For her birthday, Mrs. Lambchop had a party with a cooking theme. Stanley had given her a spatula, although he was almost injured when Arthur tried to flip him with it.

"Ah," Carlos said, nodding. "My great grandmother's secret ingredient!"

"Secret ingredient?" Stanley's mother leaned forward. "What could it be?"

"I cannot say," said Carlos.

"We promise we won't tell anyone," pleaded Mrs. Lambchop.

"I cannot tell you, *Señora* Lambchop, because I do not know." Carlos shrugged. "Nobody knows. My great grandmother guards her secret closely. There are spies trying to steal it from her always! It is sad, because when she dies, the secret will go with her."

"How old is she?" asked Arthur.

"She is a hundred and three," said Carlos, with a frown.

"That's quite young for a person over a hundred," said Mr. Lambchop.

"Carlos," said Mrs. Lambchop, "I love cooking. And this—this is the most wonderful flavor I have ever known. I would be honored to carry on the tradition of your great grandmother's secret ingredient!"

"But how?" said Carlos.

"I'll call her up," said Mrs. Lambchop.

Carlos shook his head. "My great grandmother does not have a telephone.

She lives in a very remote part of Mexico."

"I'll write her a letter!" said Mrs. Lambchop.

"She would never send her secret in the mail," said Carlos.

Stanley's mother thought for a long moment. Then, very quietly, she said, "We'll send a messenger."

"I'm your man!" Arthur leaped to his feet. He was always ready for an adventure.

But Mrs. Lambchop was not looking at Arthur. "Stanley, those red sweatpants look comfortable enough," she said. "I'll fold you some tortillas for the trip. We have to get you in the mail!"

"Aw!" pouted Arthur.

"You're sending me to Mexico?" Stanley gasped. His mother usually seemed more concerned about his health and safety.

"Stanley Lambchop, you tasted the secret ingredient," said Mrs. Lambchop. "We can not let that secret die."

"Your mother is right, Stanley," Mr. Lambchop said. "You have traveled all over the world. You explored the pyramids of Egypt."

"You practiced martial arts in Japan," Mrs. Lambchop chimed in.

"You flew on arctic winds to northern Canada," grumbled Arthur. "That was another trip I missed."

"Why, Mexico is just south of the United States of America," said Mrs. Lambchop. "That makes it practically next door!"

2

The Matador

Stanley Lambchop awoke to the sound of applause just outside his envelope. Somebody must have informed the Mexicans of his arrival!

Since becoming flat, Stanley had grown used to attention. Sometimes he did not like it, especially when strangers called him "Flatty." But he had also found that there was such a thing as *good* attention.

He remembered the reporters who crowded around him after he saved President Lincoln's nose from breaking off Mount Rushmore. He thought of the crowds calling his name as he stood with the movie star Oda Nobu in Japan. And now, he had arrived in Mexico to thunderous applause!

Stanley hoped he would have a minute to straighten himself. He liked to look presentable for his public.

At that very moment, someone tore the envelope open, and Stanley leaped out, smiling for the crowd.

But there was no crowd in sight.

It appeared that Stanley was just

outside the door of a massive stadium. The crowd must have been inside. A giant sign above the gate said PLAZA DE TOROS MÉXICO.

Staring down at Stanley was a beautiful woman in a fancy velvet outfit with a frilly white shirt. "*¿Quién es?*" she said sharply.

"I'm afraid I don't speak Spanish," said Stanley, slightly embarrassed.

"Who are you?" she repeated in English.

"My name is Stanley Lambchop," answered Stanley. "I am here for the secret ingredient of Isabela Beluga Tortilla de Sandoval." (Carlos had taught him how to properly pronounce his great grandmother's name before licking the envelope.)

"Then you are a spy!" the woman cried.

"No, I'm not!" Stanley said. "Look!" Ever since Stanley had had a difficult time at the Cairo post office, he always made sure to travel with the proper documentation. In this case, Carlos had written a letter in Spanish, explaining the situation. Stanley pulled it from his pocket.

When the woman had finished reading, she peered down at Stanley.

"You are Stanley the flat boy?"

Stanley raised his eyebrows.

"Forgive me. Carlos has been telling

me of you in letters," she said. "I thought you were in his imagination."

"You know Carlos?!" said Stanley, surprised.

"He is my cousin," the woman said, nodding.

"Then you must know Carmen del Junco, the famous bullfighter!"

The woman looked confused. Then she smiled for the first time. "I do," she admitted.

"Julio!" she called suddenly to a man nearby. She said something in Spanish and then turned back to Stanley. "You are my guest here," she said. "Julio will take care of you. I will join you after."

"After what?" asked Stanley.

Without answering, the woman opened the huge door to the stadium and slipped inside.

The crowd's roar got louder.

Julio led Stanley to another, smaller door and then through a maze of corridors. They came out among the seats of the crowded stadium. There must have been tens of thousands of people. Julio directed Stanley to a lone empty seat in the front row.

In the center of the ring was the woman who had opened Stanley's envelope. She waved a red cape in the air as a bull ran into the ring.

Stanley slapped his head with a clap: *She* was the famous matador!

The bull charged. Stanley held his breath as Carmen del Junco, the great bullfighter, calmly stepped around it, swinging her cape before its eyes. Her long brown hair flowed through the air.

The bull came at her again and again. Stanley could see the side of the bull brushing against her as it sped past.

Carmen turned and gestured up to Stanley with a flourish. She was looking right at him!

Stanley jumped up and waved. Someone in the row behind him slapped him on the back enthusiastically.

That made Stanley lose his balance. He fell forward into the ring.

Carmen waved her cape at the bull,

but suddenly it wasn't looking at her.

It was looking at Stanley.

And Stanley was wearing all red!

The bull charged. It looked much bigger, faster, and madder than Arthur. Its hooves shook the ground. Its eyes blazed.

Suddenly, Stanley felt a hand on his shoulder. He looked up and saw

Carmen. Effortlessly, she hoisted him overhead with one hand as the bull raced by.

Stanley's heart was beating so hard, his whole body was rippling.

"Smile," Carmen del Junco called up to him, as thousands of cameras flashed from the stands.

3

La Fiesta

As the sun set over Mexico City, Stanley stood in the courtyard of Carmen's home, where her family had gathered to celebrate after the bullfight. Stanley had never known a person with so many brothers, sisters, cousins, uncles, aunts, in-laws, nieces, nephews, and godchildren.

An older woman with enormous

eyeglasses rushed up and squealed at Stanley. She reached out to squeeze his cheeks, but pinched the sides of his head instead. He tried to smile.

"*Bienvenidos*," the woman cried. "*¡Bienvenidos!*"

Stanley looked around for Carmen to translate.

"*Bien* means 'well'," a voice said. It was an older boy, the first signs of a mustache sprouting on his lip. "*Venidos* comes from the verb *venir*, 'to come'. *Bienvenidos* means—"

"Well—come. Welcome!" Stanley said. "You speak English!"

"I am Eduardo," the boy said, nodding. "We are excited to meet you."

He stepped aside to reveal a group of children.

"*Está liso como un plato*," a little girl said, gasping, wide-eyed.

"She says you are flat as a pancake," said Eduardo. He grabbed Stanley and led him through the crowd.

A moment later, Stanley and Eduardo stood in a corner of the courtyard, the other children arranged around them on the grass. Eduardo said they were eager to hear Stanley's stories of adventure. Eduardo would translate.

The children ooohed as Stanley told them how he had used his body as a lever to rescue his friend Calamity Jane from a gold mine. They aaahed as he described how he had used his elbows as lethal weapons to defeat ruthless villains in Japan. They gasped when he told them he could fly like a jet plane using nothing but his muscled, aerodynamic body.

Stanley did not tell them that his brother, Arthur, had helped save Calamity Jane. He did not tell them that neither the villains he had encountered in Japan nor his elbows were particularly dangerous. And he did not tell them that he couldn't really fly like an airplane, although he sometimes got carried away by heavy winds . . . or, at moments like this one, by telling stories that weren't quite true.

It was dark when Stanley concluded his tale of the mummy he befriended in an ancient Egyptian tomb. There was no mistaking the admiration and amazement of his listeners. Someone called something out to Eduardo. The other children cried, "*¡Sí! ¡Sí!*"

"We have a surprise for you," Eduardo said, with a grin. "Come!"

They led Stanley to a grand tree. The little girl who had compared Stanley to a pancake stepped forward and held out her hands. They were filled with small candies in shiny wrappers.

"Thank you!" said Stanley. He took one and started unwrapping it.

"Not yet," said Eduardo in a low

voice. "You must put them in your pockets." Stanley did.

"Up!" commanded Eduardo, and two tall boys grabbed Stanley's legs and lifted him into the air. Above his head was a tree limb. Stanley grabbed on with both hands.

This is a strange surprise, thought Stanley. He looked down and saw the little girl standing beneath him. Her wide eyes were hidden by a blindfold. The other children started spinning her around and counting.

"*¡Uno! ¡Dos! ¡Tres! ¡Cuatro! ¡Cinco! ¡Seis! ¡Siete!*"

After seven spins, the girl weaved

with dizziness. Someone handed her a giant stick.

The girl held the stick over her head and swung it. Stanley felt a swish of

air against his leg.

"Hey!" he cried. All the children were cheering.

"What are you doing!" yelled Stanley again as the girl swung the stick a second time, grazing his foot.

"YOU'RE GOING TO HURT ME!" screamed Stanley at the top of his flat lungs.

"*¡Alto! ¡Alto!*" cried Eduardo. The little girl froze. "Is something wrong, Stanley?"

"What the heck is going on?!" Stanley said.

"We are playing piñata," replied Eduardo.

"But I'm *not* a piñata!" said Stanley.

"Now get me down from here!"

The two tall boys rushed up and helped Stanley to the ground.

"But we thought—" said Eduardo.

"What?" huffed Stanley.

"We thought you could not be hurt," Eduardo said. "From your stories . . . you seem so fearless and . . . *indestructible*. Like you are made of rubber. We thought you would *like* to be the *piñata*."

Stanley shook his head sadly. He folded himself to the ground.

"I *can* get hurt," he said quietly. "I know I didn't make it sound like I can. But I can get hurt just as easily as anyone. I should have been honest with you."

Eduardo was frowning.

"I'm sorry," Stanley said softly. He gave a heavy sigh. "All I want is to get Carlos's great grandmother's secret ingredient and return home safely."

Eduardo blinked. "Is that why you are here? For the secret of *La Abuela*?"

Stanley nodded.

"There are spies," said Eduardo.

"I know," Stanley said.

"It is very far," said Eduardo.

"I know," repeated Stanley. "But I promised I would try, and I can't turn back now."

Eduardo peered deep into Stanley's eyes. Then he walked off to talk to the other children.

They probably never want to see me again, Stanley thought.

Eduardo returned. "We will take you to La Abuela," he announced.

"Really?!" said Stanley.

"The journey is long and dangerous, even for one as fearless and indestructible as you," said Eduardo. "We will protect you."

Stanley looked up at the children who now encircled him. His heart felt warm. Silently, he reached into his pocket and began passing out candies.

4

The Mayan Temple

Stanley had traveled more than most people his age. And although he enjoyed visiting faraway places, it was not always easy. For instance, airmail was sometimes warm and uncomfortable.

But the journey to see La Abuela was more difficult than any Stanley had ever taken. On this trip, he did not have the luxury of waiting patiently in an envelope, or of being rolled up and placed on the back of a horse.

On this trip, he walked. He walked, and walked, and walked. Guided by Eduardo and three others—little Isabel with her wide eyes, and the tall boys named Esteban and Felipe—Stanley walked until he thought his legs would crumple.

Finally, on the third day, Stanley was so tired, he started seeing things.

"I must be back in Egypt," he mumbled. "I see a pyramid."

Eduardo grinned. "We are not in Egypt," he said. "That is a Mayan temple." He slapped Stanley excitedly on the shoulder. "We are getting close!"

Stanley stared up at the enormous pyramid rising out of the jungle. It was different from the ones in Egypt. It appeared that there was a giant staircase on each side. And all of the steps led to one place: a small, rectangular building on top.

Isabel ran ahead and started up the steps. Esteban and Felipe followed her.

Eduardo slowed his pace to walk alongside Stanley. "This was once a royal city," he explained. "There were roads, a palace, and aqueducts to carry water. For two thousand years, the Mayan empire stretched from here to Honduras. The Maya were scientists and mathematicians. They made a calendar that is more accurate than ours today. They figured out how long a year is on the planet Venus. Apart from ruins like these, only their descendants remain."

At the base of the pyramid, Eduardo turned and leaned in close to Stanley. "And La Abuela is one of them."

"*Pardon moi.*" A tall man with a thin mustache held out a camera to Stanley. He wore a white shirt that had two rows of buttons down the front. "Would you take my photo?" he said with a smooth French accent. "This is a very special day for *moi.*"

"Sure," said Stanley. This was the first tourist other than himself he'd seen the whole trip.

"Say cheese!" Stanley said.

But instead of smiling, the man frowned like a clown. "No, no, no," he sang. "Cheese is not the ingredient we had in mind."

Two other men emerged from the jungle—one short and fat, the other bald and muscular. Both wore the same uniform as the first man. Stanley noticed an insignia on the breasts of their white double-buttoned shirts. They looked like chefs. In fact, the bald one was holding what appeared to be a long kitchen knife.

"Spies!" realized Stanley.

Eduardo turned and sprinted up

the pyramid toward Isabel, Felipe, and Esteban. The man grabbed Stanley's arm before Stanley could follow.

"I am not a spy!" the man spat. "I am the great four-star Chef Lillou of Bourgogne! Reynaldo is my sous chef. Patrice, my saucier. We know nothing of spying. We know only cooking!"

"And carving," said bald Reynaldo ominously, rubbing the blade of his knife with his thumb.

"Why are you standing there?" Chef Lillou barked at his staff. "Get those children!"

As the saucier and the sous chef charged past, Chef Lillou turned Stanley horizontally, tucked him under his arm like a loaf of French bread, and started up the steps after everyone else.

"What is an American flat boy like you doing in this part of the world?" he said, his arm tight around Stanley.

"Just visiting." Stanley gulped.

The chef snorted. "Is that so? Well, I have been trying to visit La Abuela for nine years," he said. "Except no one knows where she lives."

Isabel screamed as, halfway up the pyramid, Patrice the saucier grabbed her by the waist and hoisted her in the air, her legs kicking furiously.

"Nine years away from my restaurant," Chef Lillou continued. "Nine years in pursuit of perfection.

But today, my persistence pays off. Because you and your friends know where La Abuela lives, don't you? She lives at the top of this pyramid. You led us right to her!"

Someone whistled behind them. Chef Lillou swung around, and Stanley swung with him.

It was Carmen del Junco!

"*Bonjour, madame*," Chef Lillou began smoothly.

"I do not think this is your pyramid," Carmen said calmly. "I do not think this is your country. And I do not think that is your flat boy." She came toward them.

Chef Lillou gave a signal. The other

spies dropped the children they were holding and charged back down the steps toward Carmen.

Carmen did nothing. Nothing, that is, except take one very small step to the left—and then to the right—and then wiggle her hips ever so slightly.

The sous chef and the saucier lunged, but missed her completely.

"Oomph!"

"Ow!"

"*Adiós*," Carmen

said as they tumbled down the steps.

Only Chef Lillou remained, with Stanley under his arm. Carmen stepped toward them.

"Please, *madame*. Come no closer!" the chef said, brandishing the upper half of Stanley's body in an attempt to ward her off.

Carmen was now less than three feet away. She winked at Stanley.

In one graceful motion, Carmen bent at the waist and grabbed Stanley's hands. She pulled him from the chef's grasp and spun around like a dancer. Stanley's feet sailed through the air. Completing their round, his shoes hit Chef Lillou square in the middle of his crisp white chest.

"Zut alooooooooors!" the chef cried as he crashed all the way down to the bottom of the pyramid.

The children cheered as the chef and his staff scampered back into the jungle.

They all hugged Carmen.

"You were wrong to go off without telling anyone," she said. She repeated herself in Spanish so that Isabel, Esteban, and Felipe would understand. Isabel's eyes welled up with tears.

"Now, you must return home. I will take Stanley from here."

"But we are so close!" said Eduardo.

Carmen lifted her eyes to the low

building at the top of the pyramid.

"It is lucky you were not closer," she said. "Or La Abuela's secret would be a secret no more."

The Plunge

Carmen waited until the other children were out of sight before continuing up the steps with Stanley.

Stanley wished she hadn't sent his friends away. "Why couldn't they come, too?" he sulked.

"Because they could not," Carmen declared.

"They were just trying to help,"

Stanley said. "They came all this way, and you made them stop just steps from La Abuela's house. It's not fair." He kicked a step hard with his toe.

"Stanley," Carmen said. "How did you become flat?"

"The bulletin board over my bed squashed me in the middle of the night," Stanley grumbled.

"Was that fair?" said Carmen.

"No." Stanley shook his head. "It wasn't fair at all. People make fun of me. They stare at me. Sometimes I wish it had been my brother, Arthur."

Carmen nodded thoughtfully. Together, they climbed the last step. Stanley took a moment to straighten

himself and flatten his hair before stepping inside to meet La Abuela.

"Hello?" Stanley called, leaning through the archway. "*¿Hola?* La Abuela?"

His voice echoed from one end of the building to the other. It was empty. There wasn't even any furniture.

"Where is she?" Stanley said.

Carmen walked across the floor. She turned to face Stanley, her silhouette framed by an archway identical to the one they had entered.

"When I was your age," Carmen said, "only boys were matadors. Even then, I knew I wanted to fight bulls. I cried very much, because it was not fair. It was not fair that I was a girl. It was not fair that I had this body.

"But then, someone very wise told me a secret. And now I will tell that secret to you: It is not what you have that matters," said Carmen. "It is what you do with it."

She beckoned for Stanley to come and look.

Stanley gasped. There were no steps down the other side of the pyramid. In fact, there was no other side to the pyramid at all. There was only a cliff that dropped from this side of the building like a huge wall, all the way down to a blue pool of water far, far below.

The green of the jungle made a blanket over the land. Stanley felt as if he could see for miles.

"So where does La Abuela live?" he said.

"I don't know," said Carmen.

"What?"

"No one has ever been able to go beyond this point to find her. I know only that the water leads to her."

"But how are we supposed to get down to the water?"

"We are not," said Carmen. "You are."

Stanley was speechless.

Carmen's dark eyes twinkled. "What

are you going to do with what you have, Stanley?"

Stanley peered over the edge. He could not float down like a kite, because there was no wind. And this was nothing like Niagara Falls, which had been an accident, in any case.

In a flash, Stanley knew what he had to do.

He took several big steps back.

"*Buena suerte*," Carmen whispered. "Good luck."

He took three deep breaths.

And then he ran and dived over the edge.

La Abuela

Stanley had seen Olympic divers on television: their bodies perfectly straight, their hands like arrows piercing the water. Stanley made himself as flat as he could. The wind rushed around his ears. The side of the cliff blurred before his eyes.

He barely made a splash.

Stanley shot toward the bottom of

the water like a bullet. Suddenly, he noticed an underwater cave to his left, swarming with fish. He went for it.

Inside, Stanley knew he couldn't hold his breath much longer. His hands broke the surface and hit the cave's rocky ceiling.

There wasn't nearly enough space for his head.

How am I going to breathe?! he thought in a panic.

Then he remembered Carmen's voice: *What are you going to do with what you have?*

Stanley swung himself into a back float. His flat body barely rose above the surface. The ceiling of the cave was

inches from his nose.

He gulped the air hungrily.

A current began pulling him along. It started gently and then got faster. Soon, Stanley felt like he was riding a water slide—except it was pitch-dark, and all the sides were covered with sharp rocks.

The current rose to a roar. He swung into the wall and scraped his leg. Stanley cried out.

Vroosh. He shot out of the cave.

Stanley found himself in a calm, clear pool of water shallow enough that he could stand.

Around the pool was a small field of herbs, planted in rows.

And at the edge of the field was a tiny cottage.

Stanley walked ashore, careful not to step on any of the plants. He was about to knock on the door when it opened.

A very small, very old woman stood before him. Stanley swallowed hard. "La Abuela?" She was smaller than Stanley was, with big cheeks and short gray hair. She wore a colorful dress and a patterned scarf around her neck.

She looked at him curiously.

Stanley reached into his pocket for Carlos's letter, but all he found was a few soggy bits of paper.

"I'm not a spy," Stanley said quickly.

Without responding, La Abuela reached for his hand. She raised his arm before her eyes and turned it this way and that, examining its shape.

Then she turned her gaze to Stanley's face. Stanley held his head high so she could look.

When he looked down again, La Abuela's eyes were moist, as if she were about to cry. Her lips quivered.

"Estaba esperándole," she said. "I have been waiting for someone like you."

Stanley was about to ask what she meant when he heard a

series of splashes—one, two, three!

"Oui!" a familiar voice said triumphantly. "We have arrived at last!"

Somehow, Chef Lillou and his spies had followed Stanley!

7

The Secret

Chef Lillou burst into La Abuela's cottage, dropping his climbing harness and his scuba tank in the middle of the floor. He looked around the dim room.

"Where is she, you little *crêpe*?"

Stanley shifted uncomfortably in his chair. "I don't know," he said, shrugging.

The chef walked over to the lumpy

bed. "You cannot fool Chef Lillou," he said. "She is hiding beneath these covers!" He whisked the blankets off. Nothing.

He held a finger in the air. "She is in the closet!" He bounded over to a wardrobe and threw it open. Empty.

"She's gone," Stanley said. "I came all this way just like you, and she's not even here." He pointed to the scrape on his leg and frowned. "Now I can barely walk."

"Do not look for sympathy from *moi*," Chef Lillou waved his hand in the air. "After that woman on the pyramid, I have more bruises than an overripe tomato." He scanned the room one more time.

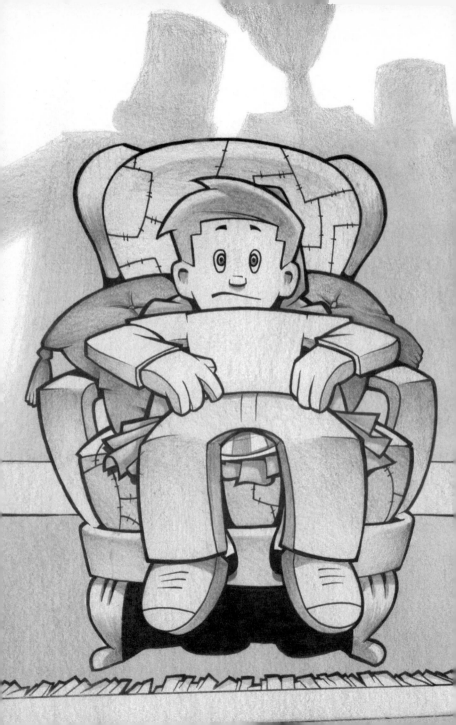

"I do not care," he said, sticking his nose in the air. "Outside is an entire field of La Abuela's secret ingredient. I have spent nine years seeking perfection, and now I have found it. I will be the greatest chef in history!"

He marched into the field, leaving the door wide open. Stanley leaned forward to see. Chef Lillou bent down, plucked a green leaf, and held it up to his nose. He inhaled deeply.

"Chef," called Patrice the saucier, "do you smell what I smell?"

The chef furrowed his brow. "This smells like common coriander."

"No, not coriander," said Reynaldo. "It is cilantro, I think."

"Coriander and cilantro are the same thing, you fool!" Chef Lillou cried. "It is the most common spice in all of Mexican cooking!

"This isn't the secret ingredient," he choked.

And with that, the great Chef Lillou of Bourgogne burst into tears.

"No, no, no, no, no," he whimpered. "No, no, no, no."

"Do not cry, chef," Patrice said as he

patted Lillou's shoulder. "We can still make a unique pesto."

"I just want to go home to my restaurant," the chef blubbered.

"That sounds like a good idea," said Reynaldo gently.

Reynaldo and Patrice put the chef's arms around their shoulders. Together, the three of them walked out of the field, to return to France at last.

Stanley waited until he could no longer hear voices. Then he carefully peeled himself from his chair and turned around.

"Are you okay?" he asked La Abuela, whom he had been covering the entire time.

She nodded, a smile breaking across her face. She burst into laughter and leaped from the chair. Together, she and Stanley did a little dance. She finished by kissing him wetly on the cheek.

Stanley pointed out the door. "So that's *not* the secret ingredient?"

La Abuela giggled. "The secret is not the ingredient," she said in her broken English. "It is what you do with it." Her eyes sparkled.

Stanley suddenly understood: It was La Abuela who had told Carmen the secret that made her a great matador.

La Abuela walked into the field and plucked a handful of cilantro from the ground. She took Stanley's hand, turned it palm up, and placed the herbs on the flat of his arm. Then she took his other arm and pressed it on top of the first.

"Now," she said. "Rub as hard as you can. I will get the salt." She ran inside.

Stanley started rubbing. His arms got hot with friction.

Suddenly, Stanley smelled something familiar. It was a smell he knew from his mother's kitchen.

It was the smell of his last breakfast at home.

Stanley breathed deeply. It was the most delicious smell he had ever known.

The Last Bullfight

Four days later, the applause was building at the Plaza de Toros in Mexico City. The great matador Carmen del Junco waved hello to her fans as red roses flew from the stands to dot the ground at her feet.

An announcer's voice boomed over a loudspeaker. *"¡Y bienvenido Stanley Llano!"*

"That's me, Flat Stanley!" realized Stanley. He was stationed behind a wooden slat door at one end of the ring. He put on his biggest grin, pushed open the door, and trotted out.

The crowd leaped to its feet.

Carmen took his hand, and Stanley gave a dramatic bow. In his new satin spandex jumpsuit, he looked like a giant piece of shiny red paper folding itself in half.

"You know, it is a myth about bulls and the color red," Carmen had said when she presented the outfit to him as a present. "Bulls can't see different colors at all. It is movement that makes them charge."

Carmen now took Stanley's other hand as the bull rushed into the ring.

A hush fell over the crowd as everyone took their seats.

Carmen winked at Stanley, just as she had before rescuing him on the steps of the Mayan temple. Then she grasped his other hand, lifted him off the ground, and gave him a little shake. The bull did not look very happy to see Stanley. Its muscles rippled. Its hooves thundered in clouds of dust.

Stanley gulped and squeezed his eyes shut.

Suddenly, a hysterical shriek pierced the air. "STOP THAT BULL!"

I know that scream, thought Stanley.

He opened one eye. With a shrug, Carmen calmly lifted him onto her shoulders and stepped aside to let the bull pass.

"YOU KEEP THAT BULL AWAY FROM MY SON STANLEY!"

And then Stanley saw: His family was in the front row! Mrs. Lambchop was standing on top of a seat, waving her hands like a trapped octopus. Everyone in the arena was staring at her. Arthur looked the most horrified of all.

"Mom? Dad? Arthur?" said Stanley. "What are you doing here?"

"You think you can go away for a whole week without calling?" cried Mrs. Lambchop.

"Your mother is right, son," Mr. Lambchop said. "We were worried about you."

Carmen shuffled slightly to let the bull pass again.

"Of course, we were worried!" Mrs. Lambchop cried. "Our boy Stanley is about to get gored by a bull!"

Arthur rolled his eyes. "Well, I think what you're doing is neat, Stanley," he said.

"Thanks, Arthur," said Stanley. It sure was good to see his brother.

"Mom, is it okay if I finish just this one bullfight?" said Stanley. "Please?"

"Yeah, Mom. Please?" chimed Arthur.

"I promise, *Señora* Lambchop," said Carmen. "I will keep Stanley safe. He is a very special boy."

Mr. and Mrs. Lambchop exchanged looks. Then, slowly, Stanley's mother climbed off her chair and sat down.

A few moments later, Stanley's toes lightly brushed the bull's back as it rushed beneath him. He squeezed Carmen's hands joyously.

Everyone in the stands went wild— even Mrs. Lambchop.

"Stay back, matador!" cried Carlos. He was standing on Stanley's bed, holding Stanley by the feet like a giant knife and swinging him at Arthur, who stood a few feet back on the floor. "Or I will chop you in half like an onion with the flat American!"

"Oh yeah, Mr. Big Chef?" said Arthur. He grabbed Stanley's hands and tugged.

"Ow!" said Stanley.

"I will never let you beat me!" cried Carlos, tugging back. "Never!"

"That's what you think!" challenged Arthur.

"Arthur," Mr. Lambchop appeared in the doorway. "Haven't I told you no playing tug-of-war in the house? You're going to stretch out your brother."

Arthur rolled his eyes. "We're not having a tug-of-war, Dad. We're playing chef and bullfighter."

"Well, that's good," said Mr. Lambchop, "because I've just received our photographs from Mexico." He flipped through the pile in his hand and held up one so the boys could see.

It was Stanley being swung through the air by Carmen del Junco as an enormous bull passed inches beneath him!

"Whoa," Carlos said.

"I told you it was cool," said Arthur.

Stanley felt his cheeks turning red. He went over to his bulletin board. He pinned the photo right next to a piece of paper on which he had written, "The secret is not the ingredient. It is what you do with it."

Stanley smiled. He felt as if he could still hear La Abuela's laugh. He

could still feel the grasp of Carmen's hands. He could still smell the secret ingredient.

In fact, it was as if that smell was wafting right down the hall and into his room.

"Lunchtime!" Mrs. Lambchop called.

Stanley, Arthur, Carlos, and Mr. Lambchop stampeded for the kitchen.

THE END

MORE AMAZING MEXICAN SECRETS!

Besides being the third largest country in Latin America, Mexico is the country with the most Spanish speakers in the whole world!

Each of the three color stripes in the Mexican flag is deeply symbolic: The green stripe represents the ideals of victory and hope, the white stripe symbolizes purity, and the red stripe symbolizes the blood sacrificed by Mexico's heroes.

Mexico is located in the Pacific "Ring of Fire," a region named for the vast amount of volcanic and seismic activity it contains, and is home to many active volcanoes, such as the Citlaltépetl (also called Orizaba) and the Popocatépetl.

Though Spanish is Mexico's official language, there are sixty more indigenous languages spoken in this country, such Huastec, Maya, Mazahua, Mazatec, Mixtec, Nahuatl, Otomí, Tarastec, Totonac, Tzeltal, Tzotzil, and Zapotec.

Every year on November 1, Mexicans celebrate a national holiday called "Día de los Muertos," or "Day of the Dead," in which they honor loved ones who have passed away. Festivities include decorating their houses

with pictures of those who have passed
and eating treats shaped like skulls and
skeletons!

Mexico is the original home of chocolate!

The border between Mexico and the United
States is the second longest border in the
world (second only to the border between
Canada and the United States), and it
spans about 1,933 miles.

Mexico's capital, Mexico City, is the second
largest city in the world by population, with
a population of about 18,131,000 people.

Read the Stories That Started It All!

A Flat Boy Can Do Almost Anything!

Stanley Lambchop is an ordinary boy. At least he was, until the night his bulletin board fell off the wall and flattened him. All of a sudden, Stanley can slide under doors, mail himself across the country in an envelope, and fly like a kite!

But flatness has its serious side, too. Sneak thieves have been stealing paintings from the Famous Museum of Art, and Stanley knows he's the only one who can stop them. Will the robbers discover Stanley's plan before he foils theirs?

Have You Seen Stanley?

One morning, after a dark and stormy night, Stanley Lambchop is nowhere to be found. But wait . . . what is that boy-shaped lump underneath his bedsheets? And where's that giggling coming from? It's Stanley and he's . . . invisible!

At first there are great adventures for an invisible boy to have. Stanley becomes an unseen helper in a bike race, on a television show, and even fighting crime! But then Stanley starts to miss being seen, and wonders if he will stay invisible forever. . . .

Stanley Lambchop Is Out of This World!

The United States has received a message from distant planet Tyrra: *Will you meet with us?* The President wants to send someone who is friendly, but also someone brave, adventurous, and clever—who better than Stanley Lambchop?

The whole Lambchop family bundles into the *Star Scout* spaceship with Stanley as Chief Pilot to voyage to far-off Tyrra. But do the Tyrrans simply want a friendly meeting? Or did they lure these intergalactic visitors for another, secret reason?

Stanley's Back and Flatter Than Ever!

Stanley Lambchop thought he was back to being a normal, round boy for good—until one morning when, out of nowhere, he seems to have gone flat. *Again.* While being half an inch thick has its interesting points, Stanley can't help wondering why he can't just be like everybody else.

But when disaster strikes downtown and one of Stanley's classmates is trapped, Stanley discovers that being different can definitely come in handy. After all, sometimes it takes a flat hero to save the day.

Stanley's In For One Magic Ride!

Stanley Lambchop doesn't realize that the old lamp he's found is magic—until he rubs it and a genie appears! Of course the genie grants Stanley wishes—fame, superpowers, a magical pet, you name it.

But the more wishes Stanley makes, the stranger life becomes. Now Stanley's adventure is a mess that will take more than just a wish to undo!

Can Stanley Save Christmas?

Stanley is astonished when a girl tumbles down the chimney two nights before Christmas. It's Santa's daughter, Sarah Claus, and she's come for help! Santa says he's not going to deliver any presents this year, and now it's up to the Lambchop family to change his mind. They're off to the North Pole—but will they be in time?

And check out Flat Stanley's Worldwide Adventures!

Saddle Up with Flat Stanley

Ever since Stanley was flattened by a bulletin board, every trip is an adventure!

The whole Lambchop family is off to see Mount Rushmore. But when Flat Stanley and his brother, Arthur, team up with a scrappy cowgirl named Calamity Jasper, their vacation turns into the Wild West experience of a lifetime. Pretty soon, they find themselves in a real tight spot—even for a flat boy like Stanley!

Ancient Pyramids Can Be Flat-out Dangerous!

Because Stanley's been flattened by a bulletin board, there are places he can get to that no one else can. So when Stanley receives a letter from an archaeologist, he travels by airmail to Egypt to help find an ancient treasure deep in the heart of a great pyramid. But what if even the flattest boy on earth can't wriggle out of this dark tomb—and the terrible mess he finds himself in?

A Flat Ninja?

Stanley and his brother, Arthur, are such huge fans of the movie star ninja Oda Nobu that they decide to send him something even better than fan mail—Stanley himself! Soon enough, Flat Stanley is in Japan, seeing the country with his idol. But when trouble surprises them, it will take a real hero to save the day.

Flat Stanley Goes North!

The Lambchops are in British Columbia, Canada, for some skiing and winter fun. But when Stanley and his new friend Nick go snowboarding—with Stanley as the snowboard, of course—they take a midair tumble just as the wind picks up . . . and find themselves in an amazing Canadian cross-country journey that might just be Stanley's wildest adventure yet!

JEFF BROWN created the beloved character of Flat Stanley as a bedtime story for his sons. He has written other outrageous books about the Lambchop family, including FLAT STANLEY, STANLEY AND THE MAGIC LAMP, INVISIBLE STANLEY, STANLEY'S CHRISTMAS ADVENTURE, STANLEY IN SPACE, and STANLEY, FLAT AGAIN! You can learn more about Jeff Brown and Flat Stanley at www.flatstanleybooks.com.

JOSH GREENHUT once mailed Flat Stanley, in costume, to a Halloween party 300 miles away. He is now married to the woman who was host of the party, and they live in Toronto with their two children.

MACKY PAMINTUAN is an accomplished illustrator. He lives in the Philippines with his wife, Aymone, their baby girl, Alison, and their pet Westie, Winter.